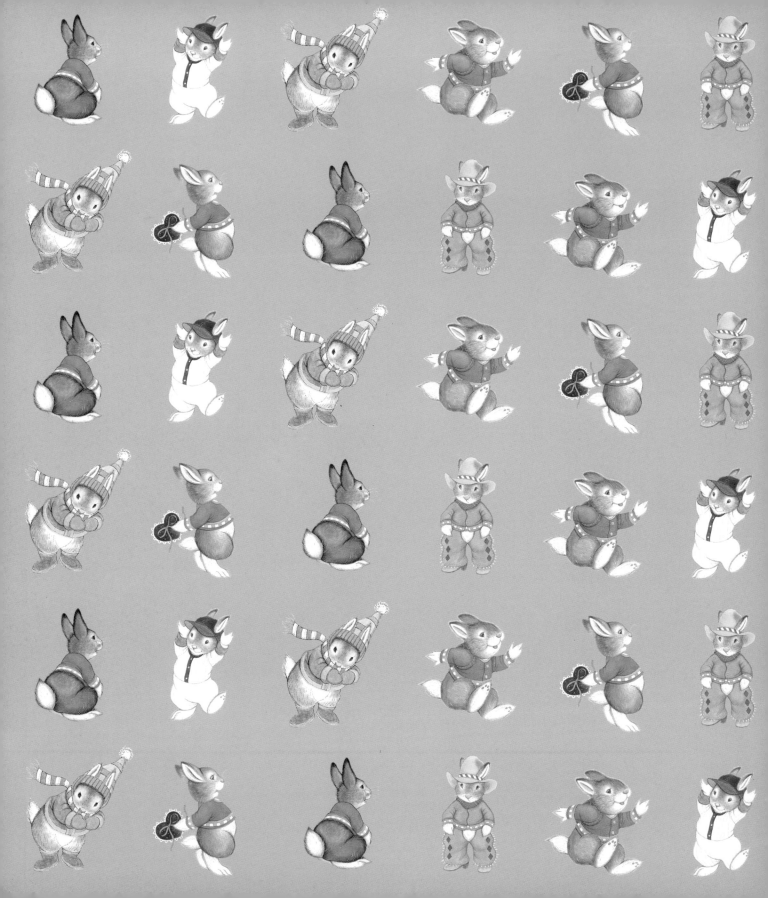

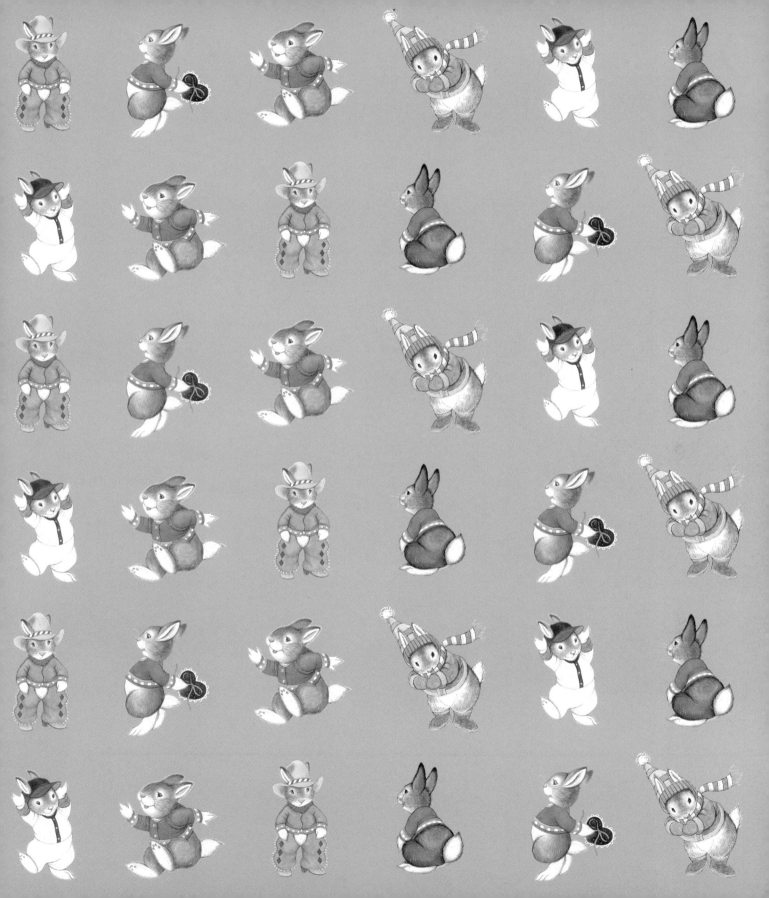

# 波波打球記

Justine Korman　著

Lucinda McQueen　繪

本局編輯部　譯

三民書局

*To everybunny who wasn't picked first.*
*It's never too late to play your best!*
*—J.K.*

獻給每一隻剛開始沒被選進球隊的兔寶寶。
表現出色，永遠都不嫌晚哦！
—J.K.

*To Jada and Bun bun, the best ballplayers on Denny Hill!*
*Love, Lucy*

獻給賈大和邦邦，
你們是丹尼山莊最棒的球員！
愛你們的露西

After a long day of teaching, Hopper the grumpy bunny was ready to go home. But his friend Coach needed to talk.

"The big baseball game between Easter Bunny Elementary and Swamp Cabbage **Primary** is coming up," Coach said with a sigh. "They don't call those **skunks** the **Invincible Stinkers** for nothing. They always win! And I just don't have enough time to coach our whole team by myself."

The grumpy bunny frowned. He didn't like the sound of this conversation!

教了一整天書，愛抱怨的波波準備要回家了。但是他的朋友康教練想和他談談。

「復活節兔寶寶小學和濕地甘藍小學的校際棒球大賽就要到了，」教練嘆了口氣說。「大家封那些臭鼬為『無敵臭小子』，可不是隨口說說而已。他們是天生贏家！而我一個人就是沒有那麼多時間去訓練我們的球隊。」

這隻愛抱怨的兔子皺了皺眉頭。他不喜歡這段對話給他的感覺！

Hopper had never been good at baseball. He'd tried to play when he was just a schoolbunny, but he was always the worst player on his team. He couldn't **throw**, **field**, or **hit**.

波波一向就不會打棒球。當他還在唸兔寶寶小學的時候，有一陣子也曾試著打棒球，但他總是球隊裡表現最差的一個。他投不好、接不牢、甚至打都打不到。

At the big **play-off**, little Hopper **struck out** in the final **inning** and lost the game for his team! The next season, he wasn't even asked to play. And some of Hopper's friends wouldn't talk to him anymore.

決賽的時候，小波波在最後一局被三振，害球隊輸了比賽！下個球季，根本沒有人願意找他去打球。而且波波的朋友當中還有些人因此不跟他說話了。

3

Coach slapped Hopper on the shoulder and brought him back to the **present**. "So what do you say, pal? Will you help the team? Will you be my **assistant** coach?"

Hopper thought hard. "Why don't you ask Marigold?" Coach's sweetheart, Marigold, was the girls' gym coach.

"Her **track** team is training for a big meet," Coach explained. Then he added, "Lilac will be assisting Marigold."

Hopper's ears perked up when he heard Lilac's name. The grumpy bunny adored the pretty music teacher.

教練拍拍波波的肩膀，這時他才回過神來。「老兄，跟你打個商量，你願不願意幫球隊一個忙？來當我的助教好嗎？」波波仔細地想了想，「你怎麼不找金花老師？」金花老師是教練的女朋友，她是女學生的體育老師。「她正在訓練田徑隊，準備參加大賽，」教練連忙解釋，接著他又補了一句，「丁香老師會來幫金花哦！」一聽到丁香老師的名字，波波的耳朵便豎了起來。這隻愛抱怨的兔子很喜歡這位漂亮的音樂老師。

"We practice Mondays and Wednesdays after school," Coach said, without waiting to hear Hopper's answer. "See you tomorrow on the field." He tossed a baseball cap at Hopper.

Hopper's paws slapped together. The cap dropped at his feet. Hopper sighed and thought, *What have I gotten myself into this time?*

「我們每個禮拜一、三放學後練習，」教練不等波波開口，趕緊往下說，「明兒個球場上見囉！」接著他丟了一頂棒球帽給波波。

波波兩掌一拍，帽子掉在他的腳邊。波波嘆了口氣，心裡想著，這次又給自己惹來什麼麻煩了？

The grumpy bunny found out at practice the next day.

"I'm going to coach the starting **lineup**," Coach told him. "I need you to work with Skip, Flip, and Trip."

As Coach led the rest of the team away for drills, Hopper looked at the three bunnies left on the bench.

"We're hopeless," Trip said quietly.

第二天練習的時候，這隻愛抱怨的兔子就知道麻煩在哪兒了。
「我要去訓練先發陣容，」教練對他說，「我需要你幫我教教『蹦蹦』、『翻王』、和『絆仙』。」
當教練把其他隊員帶開練習時，波波看著留在板凳上的三隻兔寶寶。
「我們無藥可救了，」絆仙靜靜地說。

Hopper smoothed the brim of his cap. What would Coach say? "You're not hopeless. Be hopeful! If you try your hardest, you're **bound to** improve."

"We couldn't get any worse," Flip pointed out.

Skip giggled shyly.

Hopper smiled. "From now on, you're Hopper's Hopefuls," he said encouragingly.

波波撫弄著帽緣。如果換成是教練，他會怎麼說呢？「你們還有救，要有信心！如果你們拼命努力，就一定會進步的。」

「可是我們已經爛到不能再爛了啦！」翻王一語道破。

蹦蹦害羞地吃吃笑著。

波波露出了微笑。「從現在開始，你們就是波波的『希望三人組』，」他用鼓勵的語氣說。

But the grumpy bunny soon found that it takes more than hope to hit a ball. It takes aim, skill, **strength**—and the **ability** to move without tripping over your own paws!

Hopper tried hard not to get mad at Trip when she tripped. He gritted his teeth when Skip dodged a pitch and when Flip flopped. "Let's practice some fielding **instead**," he suggested.

不過這隻愛抱怨的兔子馬上就發現打球不能光靠希望。打球得靠瞄準、技巧和力量——跑壘的時候還不能被自己的腳絆倒才行！

絆仙絆倒的時候，波波克制著不對她發飆。看到蹦蹦躲著球，而翻王又跌個四腳朝天，他也只有咬牙忍住了。

「先停下來，現在我們來練習守備吧！」他提議。

But the Hopefuls' fielding was even worse than their batting!
Flip took forever to reach the ball. Trip tripped over first base. And
Skip ran away as if the ball were going to bite him!

但是希望三人組的守備比打擊還要遜！
　　因為翻王老是追不到球。絆仙被一壘的壘包絆倒。而蹦蹦好像認為球會咬他，一看到球
就閃躲！

Finally, the grumpy bunny couldn't take any more. He threw down his cap. He was about to say "I quit!" when he heard the sound of singing from the girls' field.

Hopper saw Lilac leading the **relay** team. The runners were singing a **round** while passing the **baton**.

Lilac waved. She left the bunny-runners to their practice and came over to say hello.

看到這些景象，這隻愛抱怨的兔子再也受不了了。他丟下帽子正要說出，「我不幹了！」的時候，他聽到女生田徑場那兒傳來了歌聲。

波波看到丁香老師帶領著接力大隊。選手一面傳著接力棒，一面唱著歌。丁香老師揮了揮手。她讓兔寶寶選手們自己練習，走過來打聲招呼。

"Why are they singing?" Hopper asked curiously.

"I think singing helps the runners work smoothly together in **rhythm**," Lilac explained. "That way they'll learn to run as a team."

Hopper's ears twitched with sudden excitement. "As a team..." he repeated thoughtfully.

「丁香老師，她們為什麼在唱歌啊？」波波好奇地問。

「我覺得唱歌可以幫助選手掌握節奏，然後就能配合得天衣無縫了，」丁香老師向他解釋，「這樣可以讓她們學習到團隊合作！」

一聽到這句話，波波的耳朵猛然豎起，他突然興奮了起來。「團隊合作……」他若有所思地重覆著這句話。

Hopper returned to his Hopefuls. "From now on, forget about baseball," he told them. "Our **goal** is to become a team, and that means using our strengths to help each other."

"What if we don't have any strengths?" Skip asked.

"Everyone's good at something," Hopper **assured** him. "**For instance**, you're good at avoiding the ball. So you can lead us in a dodgeball game."

With Skip's help, Flip learned to move faster, and Trip stopped tripping over her feet!

波波回頭去找他的希望三人組。「從現在開始,別管什麼棒球不棒球了,」他對他們說。「我們的目標是要成為一支團結的隊伍,意思就是說,用我們的力量相互幫助。」

「要是我們連一點兒力量都沒有,那怎麼辦呢?」蹦蹦問。「別擔心,每個人都有長處,」波波向他保證。「比方說,你很會閃球,所以玩躲避球的話,你就可以當主將。」接下來的練習中,希望三人組在蹦蹦的幫助下,翻王移動得更敏捷迅速,而絆仙也不再被自己絆倒了!

Flip was good at juggling. So Hopper said, "Let's teach these bunnies how to catch."

At first, Skip was afraid of the falling balls. But after a while, he stopped **flinching** and started catching!

Trip had a tougher time. But she kept trying!

其實，翻王玩起拋球雜耍也很有一套。波波說，「我們來教教這些兔崽子怎麼接球吧！」
　　一開始，蹦蹦害怕迎面而來的球。但是過了一會兒，他不再怕球、也不再閃躲，而且開始接得到球了！絆仙雖然學得比較辛苦，但她不斷地練習。

"Now let's juggle together," Hopper decided.

The bunnies put on their baseball **gloves** and began to toss a ball. Flip, Skip, and Trip had always done poorly during catching practice. But this seemed different. They were playing—and having a good time!

「現在讓我們一起來拋球、接球吧！」波波決定後跟大家宣布。

兔寶寶們戴上棒球手套開始傳球。之前翻王、蹦蹦、和絆仙在練習守備的時候，老是接不好。不過這回可不同了！他們現在玩得可起勁囉！

Hopper noticed Coach's group running **laps**. He tapped Trip's arm and cried, "**Tag**! You're it!"

The grumpy bunny raced away. Trip **took off** after him. She **was** so **caught up** in the game, she forgot to trip over her feet. Instead, she tagged Flip, who started chasing Skip!

波波注意到教練那群人馬正在跑操場。他拍了一下絆仙的手臂,大喊「捉到了!換妳當鬼!」這隻愛抱怨的兔子跑開了,絆仙在後面追著。她玩得好投入,忘了自己那個隨時都會絆倒的毛病。而且她還捉到了翻王,翻王被捉到後,開始追起蹦蹦了!

A little while later, Coach blew his whistle to **signal** the end of practice. Hopper sighed. "I wish we had more time." The grumpy bunny couldn't believe what he'd just said. But it was true. He'd been having fun!

Trip agreed. "This was more like a party than a **workout**!" she exclaimed.

That gave Hopper another idea . . .

過了一會兒，教練吹哨子，練習的時間結束了。

波波嘆了口氣，「要是時間再多一點就好了。」這隻愛抱怨的兔子真不敢相信自己剛才所說的話。但是他的確玩得很開心。

絆仙也同意他的話，「我們像在開派對，而不像在練球呢！」她興奮地說。

這下波波又有了另一個點子……

At the next practice, Hopper's Hopefuls played party games. They started with "hot potato."

"Faster!" Hopper shouted.

The Hopefuls threw the "potato" baseball faster and faster.

**Eventually**, they were going so fast, they could barely see the ball. But no one dropped it!

下一次練習的時候，波波的希望三人組玩起了派對遊戲。他們首先玩「燙手山芋」。

「丟的速度再快一點！」波波大喊。

希望三人組把「洋芋」球愈丟愈快。

最後，他們傳得太快，幾乎看不到球了。更厲害的是，都沒有漏接呢！

Next Hopper brought out a **piñata**. "Remember, work as a team," he said. "The Hopefuls who aren't **blindfolded** can help the other one bat."

"What kind of candy is inside?" Flip wondered.

"There's candy inside?" Skip asked excitedly as he took hold of the bat.

接下來，波波拿出一個公雞彩罐。「記住，團隊合作，」他說。
「矇住眼睛的人在打擊的時候，另外兩個沒矇眼睛的人要幫他！」
「這裡頭有什麼糖果呢？」翻王好奇地想知道。
「裡頭有糖果？」蹦蹦拿著球棒，興奮地問著。

With that, Skip swung harder than he ever thought he could.
THA-WACK! The piñata **burst** open in a **shower** of sweets.
Skip happily shared the candy with the rest of the team. Hopper
was *very* **proud** of his Hopefuls.

握著棒子，蹦蹦用力一揮，強大的力道把自己給嚇了一跳。
劈啪一聲！公雞裂開來，灑下許多糖果。
蹦蹦開心地和其他隊友分享糖果。而波波也為他的希望三人組感到驕傲。

On the morning of the big game, Hopper's phone rang.
"It's me," a voice croaked.
The grumpy bunny knew who it was. He just didn't want to believe it.
"I'm sick," Coach wheezed. "I can't help our team beat the Invincible
Stinkers." "You can't give up now!" Hopper protested. "The team is
**counting on** you!"

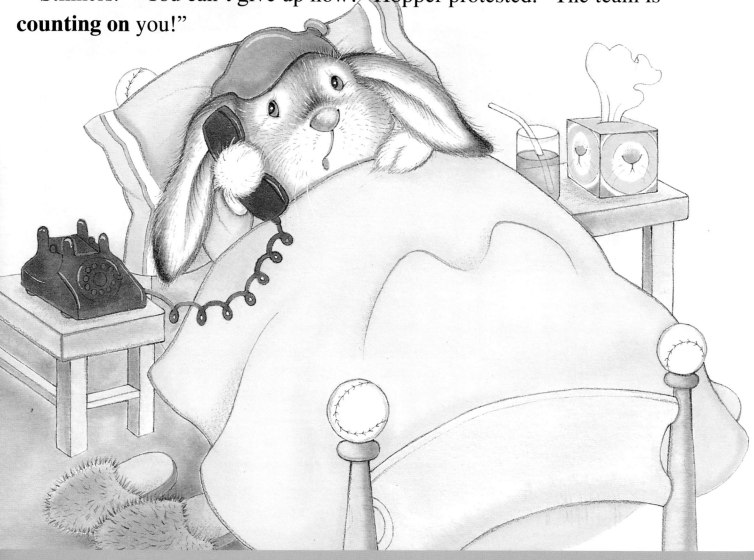

要比賽的那天早上，波波的電話響了。
「是我，」傳來沙啞的聲音。
這隻愛抱怨的兔子知道是誰打來的，只是他不敢相信。
「我生病了，」教練氣喘吁吁地說。「我沒辦法幫我們的球隊打敗無敵臭小子了。」
「不准你放棄！」波波抗議著。「我們的球隊全靠你了！」

"No, the team is counting on *you*," Coach rasped.

"What?!" Hopper squeaked.

"You can do it!" Coach said. "You'll be great. Good luck!" And he hung up the phone.

Hopper's stomach flip-flopped as he muttered to himself, "Here's another fine mess I've gotten myself into."

「不，球隊要靠的人是你，」教練的聲音變得很刺耳。

「什麼?!」波波叫了起來。

「你做得到的！」教練說。「你會做得很好的，祝你好運！」一說完，教練便掛上電話。

這時候，波波的胃翻絞了起來，他自言自語地嘀咕著，「我又給自己惹上了另一個大麻煩！」

At the ball field, the grumpy bunny's stomach **was** still **full of butterflies** as he watched the seats fill up with **fans**. *We're going to lose*, he thought nervously. Just then, Lilac arrived. She saw right away that Hopper was worried. "You'll be fine," the pretty bunny said in a soothing voice. "Just do your best." **Inspired** by Lilac's confidence, Hopper nodded. "We'll play our best—as a team!" he said enthusiastically.

在球場上，這隻愛抱怨的兔子看著座位上坐滿了球迷，他感覺到心臟七上八下地跳著。
「我們要輸了，」他緊張地想著。
就在這個時候，丁香老師來了。她一眼就看出波波不安的心情。
「沒問題的，」這隻美麗的兔寶寶安慰著波波，「盡力就好了。」
丁香的信心鼓舞了波波，他點點頭。「我們會盡最大的努力──團隊合作！」他激動地說。

At that moment, Casey the **catcher** ran up. "Pete, Sandy, and Babe have Coach's **flu**. They can't play. We'll never win without our three best players."

Hopper's ears drooped. The team was **doomed**!

Then he saw his Hopefuls waiting eagerly on the bench. "Every bunny is a 'best player,'" Hopper declared. "With Trip, Skip, and Flip, we'll do fine." He winked at the Hopefuls as he took out some baseballs. "Now get out there and toss those potatoes!"

這時候，捕手凱西跑上前來，對波波說，「彼特、珊蒂和貝比被教練傳染了感冒。他們全都不能上場了。沒有這三位最佳球員，我們是不可能贏球了。」波波的耳朵垂了下來，兔寶寶隊看來是凶多吉少了！這時候，他看到他的希望三人組坐在板凳上露出期待的眼神。「每一隻兔寶寶都是『最佳球員』，」波波鎮重地宣布。「有了絆仙、蹦蹦、和翻王，我們絕對沒問題。」他拿了幾顆棒球，對著希望三人組擠了擠眼，「走吧，咱們去丟洋芋！」

Hopper's Hopefuls played well through the whole game. Trip tripped in the **outfield**, but she juggled the ball into her glove. "Go, team, go!" the bunnies cheered.

整場比賽下來，波波的希望三人組表現得很好。絆仙在外野絆了一跤，但是她仍然奮力地把球接住了。

「加油，兔寶寶隊加油！」啦啦隊在一旁打氣。

Flip almost got **tagged out** at second base. But he quickly used one of Skip's **dodgeball** moves.

"Safe!" the **umpire** shouted.

"Yeah, team!" the fans cried.

The score was **tied** in the last inning. The bunnies had two outs. The crowd was **tense**. Who would win?

翻王差點被刺殺在二壘前。但他很快使出蹦蹦教他的閃躲絕招。「安全上壘！」裁判大吼。
「好耶！兔寶寶隊！」球迷大聲歡呼。
最後一局兩隊打成平手。兔寶寶隊兩人出局。在場的觀眾緊張得不得了。究竟誰會贏呢？

輪到膽小鬼蹦蹦上場打擊。他看起來有些害怕。
　　波波來回踱步。「為了兔寶寶隊，好好地打！」他喊著。隨後他又加了一句，「就把它當作是個公雞彩罐吧！」

**Timid** Skip was **at bat**. He looked scared.

Hopper paced. "Do it for the team!" he called. Then he added, "Pretend it's a piñata!"

Skip swung the bat so hard, he sent the ball sailing out of the park!

Easter Bunny Elementary had won the game!

蹦蹦用力揮棒,他把球打出了球場!
復活節兔寶寶小學贏了!

Suddenly, Hopper felt himself being lifted up until he rode on a **bobbing** mass of shoulders. Cheers rang out all around. Lilac smiled at him. Hopper had never felt less grumpy in his entire life!

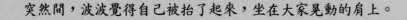

突然間，波波覺得自己被抬了起來，坐在大家晃動的肩上。

四周響起了歡呼聲，而丁香老師正對他微笑，波波這輩子從來沒有這樣幸福美滿的感覺。

Sir Byron, the Great Hare, came down from the **stands** to shake Hopper's paw. "Excellent game!" he said. "You're a good bunny to have on the team."

The grumpy bunny's ears perked up. He looked over at his Hopefuls and grinned. Hopper had finally made the team!

*It's not how many flies you catch
or times you cross home plate.
Teamwork and togetherness
make every player great!*

兔老爹拜倫先生從看臺上走下來和波波握手。「打得好！」他說。「兔寶寶隊多虧了你。」
這隻愛抱怨的兔子豎起了耳朵。他露出一口白牙對著希望三人組微笑。波波終於造就了
這支團隊。

接幾顆飛球別得意　　懂得團隊合作的道理
得分再多有啥稀奇！　　才算是真正的了不起！

ability [ə`bɪlətɪ] 名 能力

assistant [ə`sɪstənt] 形 助理的

assure [ə`ʃʊr] 動 向……保證

at bat 上場打擊

**B**

baton [bæ`tɑn] 名 接力棒

be bound to 必定的

be caught up 投入

(one's stomach) be full of butterflies 不安

blindfold [`blaɪnd͵fold] 動 蒙住眼睛

bob [bɑb] 動 上下來回地振動

burst [bɝst] 動 爆炸破裂

catcher [`kætʃɚ] 名 捕手

count on 指望，依賴

dodgeball [`dɑdʒ͵bɔl] 名 躲避球

doom [dum] 動 註定（成為壞結局）

eventually [ɪ`vɛntʃʊəlɪ] 副 最後

**F**

fan [fæn] 名 球迷

field [fild] 動 擔任內、外野手

flinch [flɪntʃ] 動 退縮

flu [flu] 名 流行性感冒

for instance 例如

glove [glʌv] 名 手套

goal [gol] 名 目標

hit [hɪt] 動 打擊

inning [`ɪnɪŋ] 名 一局

inspire [ɪn`spaɪr] 動 鼓舞

instead [ɪn`stɛd] 副 代替

invincible [ɪn`vɪnsəbl̩] 形 無敵的

lap [læp] 名 一圈跑道

lineup [`laɪn,ʌp] 名 出場選手的陣容

outfield [`aut`fild] 名 外野

piñata 名 裝著糖果、玩具等的容器《外表裝飾花樣，懸掛在高處，讓孩子矇眼棍打著玩》。

play-off [`ple,ɔf] 名 決賽，冠軍賽

present [`prɛznt̩] 名 現在

primary [`praɪ,mɛrɪ] 名 小學

proud [praud] 形 引以為榮的

relay [`rile] 名 接力賽跑

rhythm [`rɪðəm] 名 節拍

round [raund] 名 輪唱曲

shower [`ʃauɚ] 名 大量 《of》

signal [`sɪgnl̩] 動 發出……信號

skunk [skʌŋk] 名 臭鼬

stand [stænd] 名 看臺

stinker [`stɪŋkɚ] 名 發惡臭的人或動物

strength [strɛŋkθ] 名 力量

strike out 三振（過去式 struck）

tag [tæg] 動 （玩捉迷藏時當鬼的人）捉到人

tag out （對跑壘員）刺殺

take off 迅速地出發（過去式took）

tense [tɛns] 形 緊張的

throw [θro] 動 投擲

tie [taɪ] 動 平手

timid [`tɪmɪd] 形 膽小的

track [træk] 名 田徑賽

umpire [`ʌmpaɪr] 名 裁判

workout [`wɝk,aut] 名 練習

個兒不高・志氣不小・智勇雙全・人人叫好

# 我是大喜，
# 別看我個兒小小，

我可是把兇惡的噴火龍耍得團團轉！
連最狡滑的巫婆也大呼受不了呢！
想知道我這些有趣的冒險故事嗎？

探索英文叢書・中高級
Upper Intermediate

中英對照

● 大 喜 說 故 事 系 列 ●

Anna Fienberg & Barbara Fienberg／著

Kim Gamble／繪  王秋瑩／譯

每本均附CD

（本系列陸續出版中）

國家圖書館出版品預行編目資料

波波打球記 / Justine Korman 著;Lucinda McQueen
繪;[三民書局]編輯部譯.－－初版一刷.－－臺北
市；三民，民90
　　面;公分－－(探索英文叢書.波波唸翻天系列;7)
中英對照
ISBN 957－14－3446－9　(平裝)
　1.英國語言—讀本

805.18　　　　　　　　　　　　　　　90003950

網路書店位址　http://www.sanmin.com.tw

© 　波波打球記

著作人　Justine Korman
繪　圖　Lucinda McQueen
譯　者　三民書局編輯部
發行人　劉振強
著作財　三民書局股份有限公司
產權人　臺北市復興北路三八六號
發行所　三民書局股份有限公司
　　　　地址 / 臺北市復興北路三八六號
　　　　電話 / 二五〇〇六六〇〇
　　　　郵撥 / 〇〇〇九九九八——五號
印刷所　三民書局股份有限公司
門市部　復北店 / 臺北市復興北路三八六號
　　　　重南店 / 臺北市重慶南路一段六十一號
初版一刷　中華民國九十年四月
編　號　S 85595
定　價　新臺幣壹佰捌拾元
行政院新聞局登記證局版臺業字第〇二〇〇號

有著作權·不准侵害

ISBN　957－14－3446－9　(平裝)

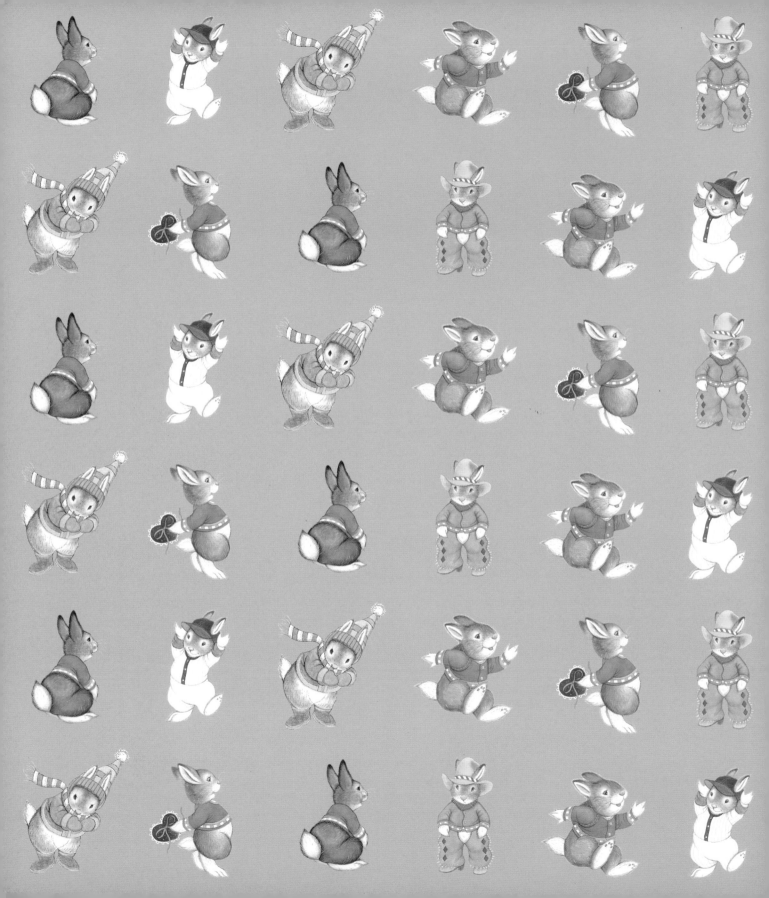

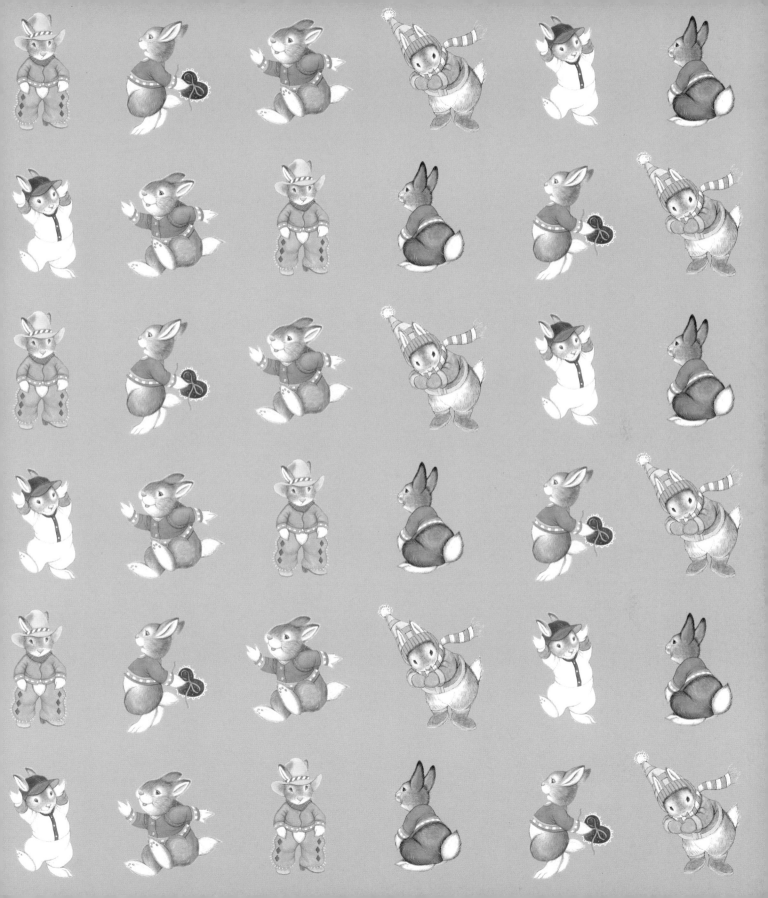